First published in Great Britain 2024 by Farshore
An imprint of HarperCollins*Publishers*
1 London Bridge Street, London SE1 9GF
www.farshore.co.uk

HarperCollins*Publishers*
Macken House, 39/40 Mayor Street Upper, Dublin 1, D01 C9W8

©2024 Pokémon. ©1995–2024 Nintendo / Creatures Inc. /
GAME FREAK inc. TM, ®, and character names are trademarks of Nintendo.

ISBN 978 0 00 861674 8
Printed in Italy
001

A CIP catalogue record for this book is available from the British Library.

Stay safe online. Farshore is not responsible for content hosted by third parties.

MIX
Paper | Supporting
responsible forestry
FSC™ C007454

This book contains FSC™ certified paper and other controlled
sources to ensure responsible forest management.

For more information visit: www.harpercollins.co.uk/green

CONTENTS

Answers on pages 36-39

Find **Eevee and its eight Evolutions** in every scene!

VAPOREON

LEAFEON

SYLVEON

FLAREON

EEVEE

JOLTEON

ESPEON

GLACEON

UMBREON

10

Sunflora Special

12 Sandy Shindig

14 Hoenn Hijinks

16 Snowy Sinnoh

18 Colourful Cave

20 River Riot

22 Let's Go Downtown!

24 Kalos Cliffside

26 Park Pals

28 Alolan Paradise

30 Coconut Chaos

32 A Galar Welcome

34 The Final Showdown

1x Gloom

6x

Let's Battle!

The Kanto region Pokémon are gathered in the stadium and ready to compete. You will smell Gloom before you spot it. Its pistils exude an incredibly foul odour! Which Pokémon do you think will beat the Grass- and Poison-type in battle?

City Escape

Five Jigglypuff are on the loose in the city. Don't fall asleep or they might draw on your face! The curious looking Jynx is also about, but there's only one of the Ice- and Psychic-type Pokémon to catch. Eevee and its Evolutions get lost in the Kanto crowd.

1x Jynx

5x Jigglypuff

5x

1x Slowpoke

Green Gathering

Welcome to the sleepy Johto region forest where a Slowpoke is getting some rest. You might think the Water- and Psychic-type is easy to find due to its slow and dopey nature, but don't be too confident! What else can you find hidden in the trees?

Sunflora Special

When the sun starts to set, Sunflora stop to soak up the final rays, but during the day they are busy little flowers! Four cute Togepi and one of its evolved forms, Togetic, are hiding amongst the happy looking Grass-types. Can you find these joyful Pokémon?

4x Togepi   **1x** Togetic

5x

2x Luvdisc

Sandy Shindig

Though the Hoenn region has a vast amount of water, it is also known for its large, dry deserts. Do you see two oddly shaped Luvdisc on this sandy plain full of Pokémon? Find them to help them get back to the ocean where they belong!

Hoenn Hijinks

It's all go here in the Hoenn rainforest with Pokémon flying, swimming and zigzagging about. You can find the Zigzagoon looking for items on the ground, and three Beautifly looking for pollen. Can you see Eevee and its eight Evolutions among this lively group?

1x Zigzagoon   **3x** Beautifly

Snowy Sinnoh

The icy mountains in the Sinnoh region are the perfect hiding place for the mysterious Froslass. Find the Ice- and Ghost-type if you can, but be careful it doesn't take you back to its icy lair! Find a cheeky Rotom as well in this snowy scene.

1x Froslass   **1x** Frost Rotom

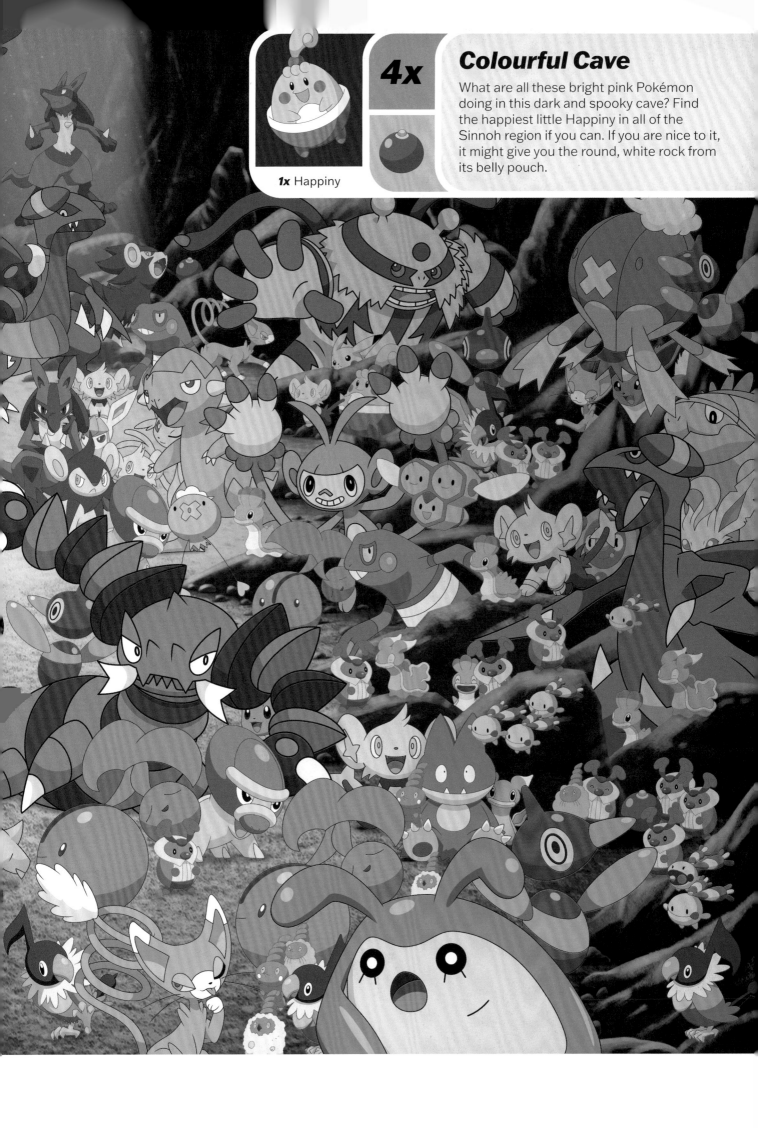

Colourful Cave

4x

1x Happiny

What are all these bright pink Pokémon doing in this dark and spooky cave? Find the happiest little Happiny in all of the Sinnoh region if you can. If you are nice to it, it might give you the round, white rock from its belly pouch.

River Riot

How many Pokémon can you see swimming in the river in the Unova region? You'll find two Stunfisk here surrounded by Sandile, then look to the sky for two Swoobat. Where are Eevee and its eight Evolutions hiding now?

2x Stunfik   **2x** Swoobat

Let's Go Downtown!

Are you prepared to face the mighty Emboar? The Fire- and Fighting-type Pokémon has taken over this cityscape, ready to throw its fire punch. Find three gentler-looking Deerling and a Watchog in the crowd.

3x Deerling   **1x** Watchog

5x

1x Litleo

Kalos Cliffside

A Noibat here, a Noibat there! The swarm are emitting ultrasonic waves to find some tasty fruit. Can you find five Sitrus Berries in this clifftop scene? There's also a cute young Litleo hanging about. Don't forget to seek out Eevee and its Evolutions.

5x

1x Sliggoo

Park Pals

This lively park in the Kalos region is brimming with awesome Pokémon pals. There are plenty of Pancham ready to battle or perhaps they are just hunting for some prey. Find the Dragon-type Sliggoo in the park – it looks a bit like a snail.

Alolan Paradise

Beware the Bewear on the islands of the Alolan Region. The pink bear-like Pokémon may look cuddly, but they are dangerous huggers! One Alolan Raichu and Rattata are hidden around the beach as well as some funky island Pokémon having a good time.

1x Alolan Raichu　　　　**1x** Alolan Rattata

Coconut Chaos

The Alola region is so sunny, that Exeggutor grows to five times the size than in any other region. These tree-like Pokémon have three heads, all of which think differently. Find some Alolan Sandshrew below the Exeggutor's long green leaves.

3x Alolan Sandshrew   **1x** Araquanid

4x

Falinks

A Galar Welcome

Eevee and its Evolutions have made it to the Galar region where some Yamper are leaping about. These dog-like Pokémon are very popular in this region and can generate electricity from the base of their tails. Can you find our adventurers in the scene?

The Final Showdown

Time to battle in the epic Galar stadium. Watch out for soaring Corviknight, cheeky Skwovet, majestic Galarian Rapidash and so many more battle-ready Pokémon. Find Eevee and its Evolutions one more time, as well as some sneaky Nickit.

6x Nickit   **1x** Sirfetch'd

ANSWERS

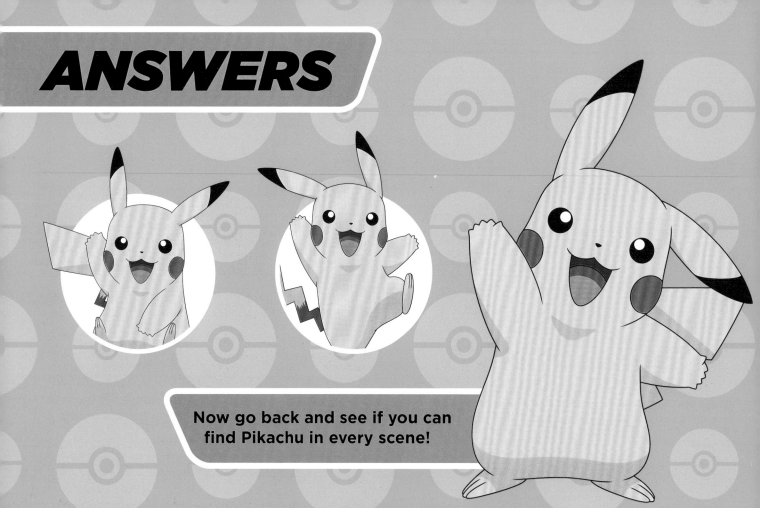

Now go back and see if you can find Pikachu in every scene!

4

Let's Battle!

6

City Escape

8

Green Gathering

10

Sunflora Special

12

Sandy Shindig

14

Hoenn Hijinks

16

Snowy Sinnoh

ANSWERS

18

Colourful Cave

20

River Riot

22

Let's Go Downtown!

24

Kalos Cliffside

26

Park Pals

28

Alolan Paradise

30

Coconut Chaos

32

A Galar Welcome

34

The Final Showdown